S]

A Novella
Featuring the Foster Family

New York Times Bestselling Author
Deborah Bladon

FIRST ORIGINAL EDITION, JANUARY
2016

ISBN-13: 978-1523635689
ISBN-10:1523635681

Book & cover design by Wolf & Eagle Media

www.deborahbladon.com

Also by Deborah Bladon

THE OBSESSED SERIES
THE EXPOSED SERIES
THE PULSE SERIES
THE VAIN SERIES
THE RUIN SERIES
IMPULSE
SOLO
THE GONE SERIES
FUSE
THE TRACE SERIES
CHANCE
THE EMBER SERIES
THE RISE SERIES
HAZE

CHAPTER 1

My mother, may her beautiful soul rest in peace forever, told me that my sins would come back to haunt me. It was wrapped in a warning about the dangers of smoking cigarettes and drinking a beer with my dad and my twin brother on our fourteenth birthday.

I didn't need the advice. I smoked one cigarette. It was a habit never formed although she believed I'd get hooked. The same was true of the beer. When I was fourteen it tasted like swamp water laced with drain cleaner. I'd raced my brother, Ben, to the washroom to see who would vomit first. I won that contest and poor Ben spent the last hour of our birthday mopping up the vile combination of alcohol and pizza that his body had expelled all over the hardwood floors in the hallway.

That was more than half my lifetime ago and since then everything in my world has changed. I'm a photographer now. The transition from taking nude photographs of women to capturing the smiling faces of children, newly married couples and the occasional celebrity was easy. Even though I work twice as hard now for a tenth of the money, I don't regret a thing. I'm proud of each picture I've taken since changing the course of my career.

I'm most proud of the family portrait I'm touching up now. I asked my former assistant, Falon Shaw, to take it on New Year's Eve. Judging by this, I could be working for her. She's got natural talent. The kind I wished I would have had at her age.

"Is it almost done, Noah? How much longer am I going to have to wait to see it?"

Her voice is my solace. Alexa Foster is my angel. She rescued me from the pit of desperation I'd buried myself in after I was stabbed. She saw something in me that I still don't fucking understand. I stopped trying to make sense of any of it the day she married me.

2

"Why weren't you this eager when I wanted to fuck you this morning?" I ask under my breath. "Your ass is my weakness, Alexa."

"My ass is your weakness?" She turns to the side to rub her hand over her jean covered ass. "Last week you said it was my breasts."

"Your tits would drive any sane man to the brink."

"The brink of what?" She winks at me. "I had to grade papers this morning. It's hard to balance the pen in my hand when you're pounding your dick into me."

I laugh loudly as I pull her into my lap. Moments like this are fleeting and rare now. After we adopted our twins, our lives took on a path of their own. I'd fallen even more in love with Alexa as I watched her help our son and our daughter adapt to a new home. Max and Chloe are happy, carefree and right now, both of my six-year-old children are on their way home with their sitter, Diana.

"I wish we had time now." I squeeze her thigh. "You don't know how badly I want you."

"I can tell." She rubs her ass over my covered erection. "I wish we had time too but the kids are almost home. When Diana called they were less than two blocks away."

There's no time for me to take her to our bed. I need it. I need to feel myself connected to her on that level before I confess to her. My wife is the only person who knows every secret I've carried with me; almost every secret, that is.

"You're on dinner duty." She taps my shoulder. "The kids are going to be starving when they get here. You should be in the kitchen."

I cling tightly to her when I feel her pull away. "Can't Diana take them out for dinner? I want to be alone with my wife."

For the first time since she's walked into our home office she looks directly at my face. Her expression shifts immediately. I can sense when realization washes over her. "What's wrong? Noah, tell me what's going on."

It would take only a few words for me to push the burden of what I've been carrying with me off my shoulders. Logically, I only need to say one sentence to explain what I've been hiding from Alexa, but I can't do it knowing our time alone is limited right now. I curse silently when I hear the sitter's key in the lock of our apartment's door. "The kids are here. I need to cook."

I kiss her softly, brushing my fingertips across her chin. The first time I saw her standing in the doorway of my penthouse back in Boston, I knew my future was with her. She's even more beautiful now than she was that day.

I've watched her cry over the scribbled words that filled the Mother's Day cards our kids gave to her and I've seen her worry over our son's mild fever one night and our daughter's bloody knee when she tripped running through Central Park. Her deep love for our family has only strengthened how much I worship her.

There was a time when I believed that my life stopped the night my body and face were scarred. Now I know that it began the day I met Alexa. I've tried to be the man she needs and wants. I've tried to give her everything, but I'm not perfect.

As I stare into her deep blue eyes, I know that once I share my news with her, she's going to question if I'm happy. She's going to wonder if the life we've built together is enough for me.

I'm Alexa's motherfucking knight in shining armor. I never want that to change. I'll do everything in my power to always be that to her, but I need to look out for me too. I can't give everything I want to her if I'm not the best man I can possibly be.

"Noah, dinner can wait." She nudges her lips against mine as her hands cup my cheek. The simple band I gave her at our wedding presses into my skin. "Something is wrong. Please tell me what it is."

I kiss her again, harder this time, wanting to feel the pressure of her lips and the taste of her mouth long after I've pulled away from her. "It can wait, Alexa. Let's go take care of our kids."

Her face brightens with the genuine smile that overtakes her. "I'll help with dinner and maybe afterwards we can go for a walk."

"It's fucking freezing outside."

"You own a jacket." Her gaze falls to my lap. "By the way, I'll take you up on that offer once the kids are asleep."

"What offer is that?" I ask through a grin.

She turns away from me as she stands, her ass wiggling in the air in front of me. "You know exactly what I'm talking about."

I resist the urge to reach out to touch her when first my son, and then my daughter, come racing into the room and into my wife's arms.

***

"Breathe, Alexa," I whisper the words into the slick skin of her neck as I pump my cock into her. "You have to slow down and catch your breath."

She nods. It's the only response other than the briefest circle of her hips against the cold tiles of the shower stall and the clawing of her nails into my shoulders.

After we'd taken a walk in the freezing cold, we'd shared a mug of hot milk with each other while the kids enjoyed the same. We'd tucked them in. Alexa reading a story about parakeets to Chloe while I told Max about the time my father took me to meet a race car driver in Los Angeles.

An hour after they'd finally fallen asleep, I'd walked away from my laptop and the dozens of family portraits I was editing from a job I had before Christmas. I wanted to give Alexa the time she needed to grade her students' schoolwork so she wasn't rushing to finish it in the morning, the way she typically does. Time management is a foreign concept to her.

It only took me a minute to realize that she was in the shower. I locked our bathroom door, shed my clothes and was on my knees in front of her in record time. I brought her to orgasm quickly, her hands woven into my hair as she stifled her desperate desire to scream as the pleasure surged through her.

My beautiful wife has learned to quiet her cries when we fuck. The only time she completely lets loose is when the kids are with her mom in Boston for a weekend or the infrequent times we meet for an hour in our bed right after she's done work for the day. I crave time alone with her. I yearn for moments just like this.

I cradle her ass in my hands, relishing the way it feels to have her legs wrapped around me. I push her back into the wall, harder with each thrust of my cock.

She tries to up the tempo again, desperate for another release. I want it to last. I want to savor each stroke of my dick inside of her.

"Slow," I whisper against her shoulder before I pull her skin between my teeth. There was a time when that slight burst of pain would result in a few harsh, heated words from her lips, but it's changed. Now, her pussy clenches around my dick as the pain races through her. The accompanying moan is soft but filled with need.

"I'm so close," she breathes.

I'm right there too. I can feel the heat pulsing through me with each grind of my cock into her. I want this to last. I want to fuck her for hours; not mere minutes but the drive to be inside of her has been haunting me all day.

Seeing her like this, barely able to control herself with her wet blonde hair framing her delicate face, and her breath restrained to muted gasps pushes me into my own release.

I cling tightly to her body as I pump every drop into her quivering pussy before I kiss her, knowing I'll capture the sounds of her climax.

CHAPTER 2

"We didn't have a chance to talk last night, Noah." Alexa adjusts the collar of Chloe's navy blue dress before she taps the edge of her still untouched plate of eggs and toast. "You need to eat this, princess, before you go to school."

Chloe pushes her dark hair back over her shoulders. It's a slight gesture but one that both Alexa and I have gotten used to. Our daughter has a stubborn streak that mirrors my own. We may have adopted them a year and a half ago, but I've never felt as though they weren't my own children. I know that we didn't conceive them, yet they are as much a part of Alexa and me as we are of each other. I can't imagine loving a child, any child, more than I love these two.

"I hate eggs." Chloe rests her fork next to the plate. "I want cereal today."

Alexa's gaze settles on Max who has already finished every bite of food that was on his plate. The kid has an appetite that never quits. I hand him another piece of toast, which he hungrily accepts.

"Your brother is eating his breakfast." Alexa smooths her hand over Chloe's hair. "If you take a few bites, I'll cut up an apple for you."

It's a negotiating tactic we've both come to rely on. It's part of the give and take of caring for Chloe. Her dark eyes dart up to her mother's face before she picks up the fork to slowly eat the now cold scrambled eggs.

"I'm sorry I fell asleep so fast after my shower." Alexa squeezes my shoulder before she walks to the counter to scoop a bright red apple into her hand. "Can we talk about it now? Is it about your work?"

I finish the rest of the coffee I poured for myself thirty minutes ago. "I'd rather talk about it when it's just the two of us."

I look up to see her staring at me. She has ten minutes before she needs to be out the door and on her way to work. If we begin this conversation now, there's no way in hell she's going to make it to class on time.

"What's your schedule like this afternoon?" She drops her gaze to the cutting board as she asks the question. "I can come right home after work."

"I've got a late afternoon shoot." I stare down at the schedule I've saved on my smartphone. "I doubt I'll make it back here before these two go to bed."

"Daddy." Chloe's on her feet, her small hands shooting to her waist. "It's your turn to read to me tonight."

"I'll do my best." I lean forward to pull her tiny frame into my arms. "Daddy will do his best to be here."

I will. I'll do everything I can to be here and to finally tell my wife what I've been neglecting to mention for the past few weeks.

**

"Do you remember taking that?" Nicholas Wolf gestures towards a framed photo hung on the wall to the left of us.

I don't need to look up from my camera to know exactly what he's talking about. I saw it the moment I walked into his loft. It's hard to miss. It's a portrait I took of a woman four or five years ago back in my penthouse in Boston. She's completely nude although the only hint of that to anyone studying the photograph is the side view of her left breast. The curve of her stomach and her hip pulls the eye in. It's a piece I'm proud of.

"The details are sketchy," I admit. "It was a long time ago."

He walks towards the large picture frame. It measures at least a few feet square. "What I love most about it is that you can't see her face. You can only imagine her beauty based on her body. What did she look like? What color was her hair?"

I finally pull my eyes to the portrait before I stare at him. He's my height but that's where our similarities end. His hair is black. His eyes a light shade of blue. I'm not surprised that he's garnering the interest he is in the literary world right now. He may be winning awards for his detective novel series, but it's his appearance that has women flocking to his book signings and television appearances. I'm not the man crush type, but I see the appeal.

"I don't remember," I answer honestly. "All their faces blurred together."

"How many women did you photograph?" He turns towards me, his arms crossing over his chest. "I once read it was hundreds."

I read that same article a little more than a month ago when I perusing the Internet one night. I'm not sure what I was expecting to find when I typed my name into the search bar. The articles and images I spent the next two hours looking at only widened the void I feel inside of me.

I don't want to go back to being Noah Foster, photographer of naked women. I don't miss the endless stream of prostitutes I invited into my home. I'd pay them a few thousand dollars in exchange for free rein to capture their nude bodies with my camera.

It filled my time and my drive to be successful. Looking back at that life now, I can see how bleak and hollow it actually was.

"I can't tell you how many." I trace my fingers along the scar on my cheek. "I didn't keep a running tally."

"Do you miss it?"

"Nope," I toss back quickly, almost too quickly.

I do miss the freedom to express myself through my art. I can't do that when I'm taking family portraits or shooting a professional head shot, like I am right now. My camera has turned into a tool I use to earn a living. It's not an extension of my creativity the way it used to be.

"You're sure?" he chuckles. "You made quite a name for yourself, Noah."

I don't answer mainly because I've got fuck all to say in response.

"That was my first purchase after I hit it big." He tilts his head back slightly towards the portrait. "I bought it last year at an auction."

I'm tempted to ask the price he paid but I know how the value of my work has skyrocketed since I retired from that aspect of my career. "It's a wise investment."

"You're telling me that?" he jokes. "Every time I look at it I'm reminded of how far I've come. I first saw your work in a gallery five, or six years ago. I didn't have two pennies to rub together back then."

I'd guess he's twenty-seven or twenty-eight which are only a few years younger than me but right now I feel like the wiser, older brother to this kid. He's living in a loft in SoHo that's either a truckload of money to rent each month or cost him a bloody small fortune to buy.

He bought one of my portraits along with a few pieces from some current all-stars in the art world. He's got an eye for beauty and a penchant for expensive things. It's obvious he's got the world by the balls right now. He reminds me of myself before the stabbing.

"Don't lose sight of what's important, Nick," I offer even though I know I have no place giving him advice on anything. "I did that for a time. It fucked me up."

"My family won't let me." He eyes shoot to mine. "I'm keeping it all in perspective, Noah. I know what matters."

I do too. What matters more than anything is my family and regardless of what I may think I need out of life, nothing can compare to what my wife and my children give to me. I need to heed my own advice and keep that in perspective.

CHAPTER 3

"Sit on my lap." I tap my fingers on my thigh.

"You sound like that Santa Claus we saw last month at the mall." She yanks the hem of her skirt up so I can see the top of her stockings. "Remember how he wanted me to sit on his lap after the kids had their picture taken with him?"

"He was a fucking pervert, Alexa." I run my hand over the smooth skin of her thigh. "You gave him a raging hard-on. You were wearing this exact outfit."

She raises her eyebrow. "How do you remember things like that, Noah?"

"I remember every moment I get to spend with you," I say it without hesitation. "I'll remember every moment we have together until the day I die."

I should know by now that words like that bring tears to her eyes immediately. Today is no exception. She covers her mouth with her hands in an effort to hold off a sob.

"You're too romantic," she murmurs quietly. "I love when you talk like that."

I pull on her waist until she's settled in my lap. "It's the truth, Alexa. I'll never get enough of you. You already know that."

She nods her head faintly. "I've been worried about us…about you, Noah."

I kiss her cheek, scooping up a tear onto my tongue. "Don't worry about me. I'm fine."

Her eyes stay trained on the wall of my office where a framed picture of our twins is hanging. I'd taken the photograph the first day they came to live with us. I can see the trepidation in their expressions. They were unsure what they were stepping into. Since then, any vulnerability that may have been hidden behind their eyes has vanished. The picture is completely out of place now. I make a mental note to replace it with our family portrait tomorrow.

"Have you been thinking about a baby again?" Her voice is soft in the stillness of the room. I can hear every hidden nuance in her tone.

She's not actually asking if I've given any thought to the idea of adopting an infant. She's telling me, in her own abstract way, that it's all she's been thinking about. I don't need to hear the words to understand that. I see it in her expression when we're out and she's gazing into the distance at a couple with a baby in a stroller. I see it in her hands as they tremble when she wraps gifts for our friends and her co-workers who are expecting a child.

Alexa has never gotten over the fact that she can't physically have a baby of her own. After we adopted the kids, she sought out the advice of yet another fertility specialist who reiterated what the previous two had. My wife will never carry a child of her own in her body. It's not meant to be.

"I haven't been thinking about a baby," I say honestly.

"Oh." She clears her throat. "I just assumed."

It's one of the very few subjects that we can't talk openly about. I love our family exactly as it is. She had mentioned a baby briefly after we adopted the twins but the subject was mute until my brother Ben, and his wife, Kayla had a baby. Alexa adores their daughter, Emerson, and it's rekindled her desire to adopt an infant.

I wanted the same thing for a time but now that the twins are settled with us, I like things just as they are. That's not to say that I won't want another child in the future. I won't rule it out but I'm not ready right now.

"You know how I feel about that, Alexa." I wrap my arms around her, tugging her into my chest. "I like our family exactly the way it is."

"I know." She swallows. "I love our family, Noah. Sometimes I just wish we had another child."

It's an issue we're not going to resolve tonight. We both know that. We revisit it on an almost weekly basis and at some point we'll have to figure it out.

"How did work go today?" I move
the conversation in a completely different
direction, hopeful that I can eventually
steer it to where I need it to be. I have to
tell Alexa about Boston. I need her to
understand why I've done the things I have
every time I've gone back there the past
two months.

"Work was fine." She brushes her
fingers against my cheek. "It's always fine.
I just finished winter break and I'm already
looking forward to the week I get off this
spring."

I could easily launch into a lecture
about how she doesn't need to work
another day in her life, but I know how
well that will go over. Alexa is fiercely
independent and she worked damn hard to
get her teaching degree.

She cut back her hours for months
after the twins arrived but when the school
asked her to take on a fuller schedule, she'd
jumped right back in. The fact that we
found an incredible sitter helped. Alexa
vetted dozens of candidates until she found
Diana.

She's a retired teacher herself with two grown children and three grandchildren. The woman has for all intents and purposes taken on the role of a surrogate grandmother to our kids. She's a gem and I pay her a tidy sum each month to make sure my two beauties are given the best care possible.

We asked her to move in the spare bedroom in our apartment but she was adamant about keeping her own place in Queens. She lives in a rent controlled studio suite there filled with the treasures of an entire life devoted to kids.

Alexa brings home gifts from her students too. The difference between her and Diana is that she packs them away in a cardboard box. Diana openly displays every colored picture, each note and every key chain her students made for her over her thirty-year career.

"I asked my dad about staying with the kids next weekend." I bury my face in the warm skin of her neck, breathing in the scent that is uniquely her. "I want to take you away."

"Where?" She spins so quickly on my lap that I lose my grip on her waist. "Are we going somewhere romantic?"

"Boston," I blurt out because there's no fucking way I'm going to give her the chance to suggest another location. If she did that, I'd drop my own plans to take her wherever it is. I'd give my wife the moon if I could figure out a way to lasso it and drag it down to earth.

"Why?" She eyes me suspiciously. "We're not going to see my mom, are we?"

"I take it you'd prefer if we didn't?" I joke. "We can hang out with her for a couple of hours if you want but I've got other plans."

"What other plans?" Her entire expression shifts. "There's nothing left for us there other than my mom."

This is it. This is where I tell my wife that I haven't been able to do the one thing she's been asking me to do since the day we married.

"My penthouse is there." I tighten my grip on her, hoping that she'll find some comfort in my touch. "I want you to go there with me, Alexa."

"It's not your penthouse anymore, Noah," she says bluntly. "At least it won't be next month when the new owner takes possession of it."

"I didn't accept that offer," I finally admit. "The buyer wanted an extension to get financing in place and I didn't give it. I shut the deal down two weeks ago."

She scrambles to her feet. Her hands pushing at my shoulders, her fingernails digging into my skin through the fabric of the t-shirt I'm wearing. "What? What are you talking about?"

I stare up at her. Her eyes are welling with tears although she's doing everything in her power to hold back the onslaught of her raw emotions.

That penthouse has been a fundamental part of my life since I bought it when I was twenty-five-years old. I'd used the inheritance that my mother left me and I'd built my career there. I also hid from the world there. It's the place I met Alexa and the same place I broke her heart. It's as much a part of me as my name. Giving it up wasn't as easy as I thought it would be.

"You've been going there to clean it out."

"No," I admit easily. "I've been going there for another reason."

"What reason?" Her hand bolts to her chest. "What are you doing in Boston?"

There's no one word answer for that. I want to show her. I want her to understand what keeps pulling me back there.

"I've been working." That's the most succinct way to describe it.

"Working?" Her voice is louder, her tone more demanding. "You're always telling me that you have too much work here in New York, Noah. You've been turning jobs down. Why in the hell are you leaving us to go there to work?"

"Not that kind of work." I stand. "I'm not taking on jobs, Alexa."

I just need to say it, but the words aren't going to come easily. Each time I go back to Boston, I lock myself back in that penthouse the way I did before Alexa came into my life. It's a safe place for me. It's the place I need to be while I sort through the remains of a part of my past I don't want to let go of.

27

"Oh, my God." She steps back, her hand reaching for the edge of my desk. "Noah, tell me right now that you're not taking nude pictures of women again. If you are, I swear that I'll…"

"Seriously?" I step towards her, my hands grabbing hold of her shoulders. "You think I'd go back to that fucked up life? I'm a father, Alexa. I have children. I have you."

"What does that even mean?" she asks defiantly, her chin tipping up towards me. "You have me and yet you've been lying to me for weeks. You said you were going back there to take care of things at the penthouse."

"I was." I drop my hands from her, pushing them into the front pockets of my jeans. "I was taking care of things."

"Riddles, Noah." I see the pain, mixed with anger as it washes over her expression. "Stop fucking talking in riddles. What the hell is going on? You tell me right now."

I swallow hard. I feel my jaw clench. "It's my mother, Alexa. I'm going back for her."

28

CHAPTER 4

We've stood in silence for more than three minutes. I know because I've watched the seconds tick by on the clock on the wall behind where Alexa is standing. I've been waiting for her to respond. I wanted her to tell me immediately that she has an understanding of what I'm talking about but it's obvious that's not going to happen.

My pretty little wife can't even make eye contact with me right now. I know her well enough to sense that's because death makes her uncomfortable. It's a subject she avoids at all costs.

"I'd like you to come to Boston with me so you can understand what I'm doing there."

"Does Ben know about this?" Her gaze doesn't move from where it's glued to the floor. "Have you told him what you're doing?"

I haven't even fully explained it to her yet. How the hell can I mention it to my twin brother? I blamed him for years for our mother's death. I can't exactly call him up and tell him that I'm creating an exhibit of photographs I took of our mother before her death so I can show them at a small gallery in Boston. That's not something you bring up over a drink at a bar.

My mother's death still haunts Ben. I saw that firsthand when we were establishing the Foster Foundation, a charity dedicated to our mother's memory. It tore Ben up inside every time I mentioned how proud she would be of him and the good work he does at the hospital.

His life is settled now. He's happy. He's married to my wife's best friend, Kayla, and he's raising a little girl. I can't fuck that all up by telling him that I can't let my mother's memory fade away.

"I told you first," I explain calmly. "I want you to come and see what I'm doing before I talk to Ben."

"What are you doing?" The question carries the perfect balance of anger and frustration. She's pissed that I didn't correct her when she made the assumption that I was going to Boston to close the deal on the penthouse.

"I was cleaning out my things," I begin as I motion towards a chair a few feet away. "Why don't we sit, Alexa? I want to explain all of this to you."

She fidgets on her feet. "She's been gone for a long time. I don't understand what's going on."

I ignore her inability to stand still as I lower myself back into my office chair. I need the stability of that to ground me so I can get through this conversation. The kids are due back with Diana sometime in the next hour so I need to get this off my chest before they burst in.

"Tell me, Noah." Her voice carries all the impatience of her movements. The toe of her left shoe is tapping a rapid beat on the floor.

"I wish our kids would have known her," I begin because that's exactly where this all started for me. "It kills me that they'll never get the chance to know her the way I did."

That quiets her enough that she sits her ass down on a chair across from me. "I'm sorry about that. I wish I could have known her too."

"That's another part of it." I scrub my hand over my forehead. "I've got this perfect family and she'll never see that. She's never going to know the three of you."

You'd think I'd be over this by now. I'm in my thirties. She died when I was eighteen-years-old. I struggle to recall the sound of her voice sometimes or the way she moved when she walked. I know her favorite flower was a rose, but for shit's sake I can't push myself to remember if I told her I loved her before I left for a ball game the day she took her last breath.

She was sick. She was really sick and if I would have been paying more attention than a teenager in search of his next high or his next lay is, I might have actually spent more time with her. I didn't. I regret it now that I see Alexa with our kids. My mother was just as giving and supportive to me and my brother as my wife is to our kids and I doubt like hell she knew how much that meant to me.

"I started sorting through my stuff there when I first put the place up for sale." I talk quickly, the words spilling out. "That's when I found boxes and boxes of old pictures I'd taken."

"Pictures of your mom?" she asks quietly.

"Her, my dad, Ben, friends." I shake my head faintly. "My folks got me a camera for my tenth birthday and I went hog wild with that thing. I took thousands of pictures."

"I'd like to see them."

Of course she'd say that. Alexa may not have been the biggest fan of my work when we met but since then she's been nothing but supportive. She'll sit next to me at this desk, grading papers while I edit images. She's learned what works and doesn't work in terms of shading and angles. I know her interest isn't coming from her own natural desire to take pictures. She's wanted to learn more about my business because of how much it means to me.

"Come to Boston with me this weekend." I lean forward to cup her face in my hands. "Come with me so I can show you exactly what I've been doing."

Her eyes graze over my face before they settle on my lips. "You know I can't resist you, Noah. I'd follow you to the edge of the earth if you asked me to."

"I'd do the very same for you, Alexa. I'd do anything for you."

***

"You said you'd do anything for me," she hisses the words from between her teeth. "You need to let me finish what I started."

I need to fuck her before I blow my load all over her face. "Stop, Alexa. I told you to fucking stop."

This is one of the few times when I can say I don't give a fuck that she's not listening to me. I'd gone to bed before her but when she crawled in next to me, all bets were off. Sleep was the last thing on my mind when she took my dick between her lips and sucked me to the back of her throat.

I'd almost lost it right then. I had to physically pull her off of me so I could catch my breath. She wasn't having it though and with a few quick flicks of her head to free her hair from my hand, her mouth was back on me, sucking, licking, taking me to the edge over and over again.

I want to come down her throat. I want that almost as much as I want her to climb on top of me so she can ride me.

"Get on my cock," I pant the words out quickly as she slowly licks the underside of my dick. "I want your pussy."

35

She moans as she scrambles hastily, shedding the boy shorts and tank top she's wearing. She'd turned the small light on the nightstand on when she walked into the bedroom and locked the door. It's enough of a glow to highlight her beautiful body. My cock stiffens even more as my eyes trail over her.

"Ah shit," I murmur as I watch her glide her long fingers through her soft folds. "You're ready."

"Sucking your cock turns me on." She dips a finger into her channel, pulling it out and over her swollen clit. "I love sucking it."

She stands on the bed, straddling me while she continues fingering herself. I stare up, in awe of how incredibly fucking beautiful she is; in disbelief that this woman agreed to spend the rest of her life with me. This is mine. All of this is mine.

"Sit on my face. Let me taste you." I fist my cock, bringing myself to the edge again.

"Not a chance." She's down and on me in an instant, her hands pulling mine away from my dick. "I'm going to come with this inside of me."

I stare at her face, watching her eyes flutter closed as she slides my shaft into her very wet, very ready pussy.

CHAPTER 5

"If I fall asleep in class today, it's your fault." She rests her hands on my shoulders as she reaches up to kiss my cheek. "You're a fucking machine, Noah."

"A fucking machine?" I parrot back. "You've never called me that before. Does that mean you like me, Mrs. Foster?"

She rolls her eyes as she purses her lips. "Only my students call me that."

"You didn't mind when I called you that last night." I arch my brow.

She kisses me softly, her tongue grazing a lazy path over my bottom lip. "You can call me whatever you want when we're in our bed."

"Whatever I want?" I ask in a soft voice when I hear the twins rounding the corner to come into the kitchen. "I'm going to remember that. In fact, I'll never forget that."

The sudden curve of her brow is a silent question but I'm on dad duty now. That means I've got to find something, anything to get in front of Max before he eats his plate, and I have to coax my beautiful brunette little princess to eat a few bites of banana before I take them both to school.

"When's grandpa coming over?" Max walks right past me on a mission to get to the refrigerator. He opens the door with both hands before he pulls out a small tub of yogurt. "I have some stuff to go over with him."

"Go over with him?" I reach behind me to yank open the utensil drawer before he reaches it.

He grabs hold of a spoon and then closes the drawer with his shoulder. "We're working on something. I called him but he didn't get back to me yet."

This kid is way too smart for his own good. "When did you call him?"

"What time was that, Mommy?" He sits by the kitchen table, as he pulls off the lid of the yogurt. He runs his tongue over it before he drops it on a paper napkin.

Alexa smiles as she stares at him.
"You called him last night around seven,
Max. I told you grandpa was traveling
yesterday to Texas. I'm sure he'll call us
back tonight."

"You'll tell me right after school if
he called you, right?"

I feel like I'm sitting on the sideline
of a tennis match as my wife and son
volley responses back and forth. Chloe has
settled in a chair by the table as she takes
the smallest bites humanly imaginable of
the banana Alexa peeled for her.

"Grandpa might call me," I
interject. "I am his son after all. You
haven't forgotten that, have you?"

Max laughs. It's like warm sunshine
as it bounces off the walls of the kitchen.

"What's so funny?" I crouch next to
him, burying my index finger in his side.

It brings up an even bigger giggle
as the yogurt that was in his mouth seeps
out the sides. "Grandpa always calls me on
Mommy's phone. You know he does."

I do know that. I know that my father talks to Max on an almost daily basis and I couldn't be more grateful that he's as committed to spending as much time with the kids as he is.

"I'll call him this morning and tell him to come to New York next week," I offer not only for Max but also for myself. I miss my dad.

When I stopped taking nude photographs of women, he lost his job as my manager, which meant he was officially retired. He now spends his time golfing, jetting around the country to visit friends and spending time with his grandchildren. He's been on his own since my mom died. He's dated a few women but not one of those relationships has gone very far. He says he's happy being alone. I have no reason to doubt him.

"Tell him to hurry, Daddy." Max brushes his hand over the tattoos on my arm. "I need to tell him something very important."

***

"Did you sell your place in Boston yet?" My brother tilts his chin towards an empty table in the hospital's cafeteria. "I'm thinking of listing the condo I've got there. I may wait for the market to swing back up."

I settle onto one of the extremely uncomfortable plastic chairs that litter the space. It's mid-afternoon so the lunch crowd has thinned enough that a person can actually move. I meet Ben during his breaks whenever I can, but he knows not to ask me here between eleven and two. I've made that mistake before and I won't again.

"It hasn't sold." I take a sip of the bitter coffee. "How's Kayla? Tell me about Emerson."

When Ben and his wife first told me they were naming their daughter after our mother I had to bite down the urge to cry. I had imagined doing the same thing after her death, but when I saw Emerson Foster for the first time, I knew the name belonged to only her. She's a perfect mix of my brother and his wife.

"She's great. They're both great." He leans back on the chair, crossing his legs. "What's going on with you?"

"Nothing," I lie. "Working hard, hanging with my kids, chasing my wife. You know how it is."

He raises his hand to wave at someone behind me before his gaze falls back on my face. "You've got something going on. I can see it in your eyes. I heard it in your voice when you called me this morning."

"Bullshit." I chuckle. "I've got nothing going on."

The expected laugh doesn't come. Instead, he pulls his teeth across his bottom lip. "You've been thinking about mom, haven't you?"

Some people would call that twin intuition but that's not what this is. He's not using a special sibling power to read my mind. He's fishing and I know exactly why. "You're asking me that because it's her birthday in two weeks."

"It would have been her birthday in two weeks," he corrects me. "I've been thinking about that too."

I pick up the paper cup of coffee and bring it up to my lips. It takes like shit but it's worth it if I can avoid discussing this subject with him today. I don't want to delve into an emotional conversation about our mom in the middle of the cafeteria.

"We should hang out that day." He taps the toe of his shoe against my leg under the table. "We can have some beers, shoot some pool. We should do something to commemorate the day."

"Take the day off, Ben. Meet me in Boston."

He doesn't say anything at first. He stares at me, his eyes widening as if some realization has suddenly washed over him. "Done. I'll fly out that morning."

I smoothly shift the topic to the weather. The details of what we're going to do that day don't matter one bit. My twin brother and I are going to honor our mother on what would have been her 60th birthday.

CHAPTER 6

"Part of me hates when you do that, Noah." She tosses those words over her shoulder at me without even a backward glance. "You come in here and look like the hero."

"I am the hero." I cross my legs at the ankles as I rest against the edge of her desk. "Your students fucking love me, Alexa."

She turns towards me, her hands darting to her ears. "Don't talk like that here. I teach eight-year-olds, Noah. No swearing."

I wave both my arms in front of me in a grand gesture. "Your students were dismissed thirty minutes ago. The only one who can hear me swear is you."

"That's not the point."

I love when she's like this. She's in full-on teacher mode including her outfit. She's wearing a red pencil skirt and a white blouse, buttoned right up to her neck. She's the definition of prim and proper to anyone looking at her. I know the woman beneath the clothing though.

"What's the point?" I ask through a grin. "You like when I talk like that to you."

"Noah, please," she does her best to sound exasperated because it comes out all kinds of sexy instead. "Don't say fuck in my classroom."

I've learned, through much painful and aching trial and error, to control my body around my gorgeous wife. That's not to say that the constant ache inside of me to be close to her is any less now. I've just matured to the point that I can hold off until we're alone together in a place that preferably isn't in the middle of a school.

"You're tempting me, Alexa," I growl. "You're teasing me now."

"Am I?" Her hands leap to her hips. "Is that what I'm doing?"

I'm a millisecond away from grabbing her and bending her over her desk when we both turn towards the sound of footsteps in the hallway. A woman scurries past the open door, her arms loaded with books.

"You best behave." I warn my wife with a wag of my finger in the air. "You don't want to get sent to detention."

"Enough with the kinky school talk." She giggles. "It was actually very kind of you to bring the students those photo books, Noah. You know how much they love seeing you."

"I love seeing them too."

It's the truth. I've tried to stay semi-involved with each class that Alexa's taught since we became engaged. She goes out of her way to give her students a full experience including buying supplies out of her own pay check. I stop by at least a couple of times each semester with a gift in hand. Sometimes, I get them new coloring markers or sketch pads. Today it was a photo book that a friend of mine published last year for kids. I bought every copy the store had in stock. Tomorrow I'll deliver the ten I have left to the community center I used to volunteer at.

"I heard that you're going to Boston with Ben on your mom's birthday."

Awkward news travels fast. I left the hospital less than two hours ago. My brother must have my wife on speed dial.

"Ben called you?" Clarification isn't necessary. It's a simple stall technique. As much as Alexa hates dealing with anything death related, I know it's got to sting that I'm spending a day like that with anyone but her.

"Kayla." She busies herself with straightening a pile of papers on her desk. "Your mom would have been sixty-years-old that day."

It's a foreign concept to me. I remember my mom as a vibrant woman who loved working in her garden and volunteering. It's hard to imagine her as a grandmother in her sixth decade of life.

"I'll only be gone for the day, Alexa. I'll be back first thing the next day."

She crosses the room quickly until her hands are resting on my chest. She fiddles with one of the buttons on my blue dress shirt. "You take all the time you need. I want you and Ben to spend that time together. I know it's important for you both."

I married the most perfect woman in the world. How the fuck did that happen?

"We're still going to Boston this weekend, right?" I ask as I scoop her hands into mine. "You haven't forgotten about our trip, have you?"

She studies my face, her eyes resting on my scar. "The world's most handsome man invited me away for a weekend. I wouldn't miss that for the world."

***

"We should have picked up a sandwich at Axel Boston on our way over." She's literally doubled over in laughter from her own joke. "How funny would that have been?"

I rest both of our overnight bags on the floor just inside the door of the penthouse before I close it behind me. "You know how much I hate sandwiches, Alexa. What the fuck?"

That brings up a snort. A very loud, very sexy, snort. Tears flood her eyes. "Do…do you…Noah, you remember…"

"What?" I grab hold of her waist. "Do I remember that I had a raging hard-on when you brought me a sandwich the first time?"

"Oh, my God." She slaps my stomach. "No. I wasn't going to say that."

"You couldn't keep your eyes off my dick." I tilt my chin towards my groin. "If memory serves me, you drooled all over this floor. It was right here. You may have ruined the finish of the floor there was so much drool."

Tears stream down her face now. "No. I wasn't. I didn't drool."

"Oh, you drooled." I pull the scarf that's around her neck free before I slip her wool coat off her shoulders. "You were panting too. I remember the panting."

The giggles have taken over now and there's no end in sight. She holds tightly to the arms of my coat. "You never…you didn't…you had no clothes on."

"No clothes?" I arch both brows. "Good idea."

She straightens and the laughing comes to an abrupt halt as I push my coat off, pull the sweater I'm wearing over my head and lose my shoes, jeans, socks and boxer briefs in twenty seconds flat.

Her eyes flash over my legs, across my cock and up my firm stomach before they settle on the tattoos that cover my chest and arms.

"Noah," she whispers as her right hand darts to my forearm and then up my shoulder. She silently traces the outline of my tattoos with her fingers, lovingly stroking the lines. Her fingers float over the scars that are hidden beneath the colorful canvas of my skin. "You're so beautiful."

I've never told her how much those words mean to me. Alexa has never looked at my body or my face with anything other than love and desire.

The scar that transcends my cheek draws stares on a daily basis but it's all muted the moment I step into our apartment and her eyes lock with mine. I see myself the way she does now. I'm everything to her. It's more than I ever thought I could be.

"You're the beautiful one." I yank on the hem of the sweater she's wearing. It's bulky and does nothing to highlight her body but she wanted something warm to wear since it's freezing outside. "Even in this sweater you're still the most gorgeous thing I've ever seen."

That reignites her laughter. "You bought me this sweater."

"Bullshit," I say as I pull it over her head. "I wouldn't buy you something that looks like this."

"Technically," she begins before I unbuckle her jeans. "The kids picked it out for my birthday and you paid for it."

"Their fashion sense is crap." I shake my head. "Doesn't look like either of them is going to work for my cousins running the fashion empire they've built."

She laughs even harder at that. "Maybe they'll be photographers."

"Max is going to be president." I push her jeans down slowly. "Chloe has some options. She'd make a great lawyer. She's got the composure for it."

"Maybe Chloe will be president." Her hands rest on my shoulders as I kneel down to help her take off her boots. "I want them to be whatever they want to be."

I look up and into her face. "They'll be exactly who they're meant to be. We'll both make sure of that."

"You're the best dad in the world, Noah." Her bottom lip trembles slightly. I can't tell if it's from the chill in the apartment or her emotions. "I'm glad you're my children's father."

"I'm honored to be their father." I kiss her knee. "I'm grateful to be your husband."

With those words, she lowers herself to her knees, wraps her arms around my neck and kisses me deeply.

CHAPTER 7

She woke up before me. That's exactly the opposite of what I wanted. I'd picked her up after I finished undressing her and I'd carried her to the bed we first made love in. We spent the next few hours wrapped in each other's arms, fucking, talking, sharing.

The last time Alexa and I were here together, I was afraid to leave this place. Now, as I wake to the bright sunlight pouring in through the open curtains, I realize it's not the place I'm afraid of letting go of, it's the memories.

I swing my long legs over the side of the bed. I don't even consider finding something to put over my naked body. I need to find my wife. I need to explain what I've been working on.

I'm too late. I realize it as soon as I walk into the hallway and see the door to my office wide open. I used to lock it when I left here, as if the gesture itself would somehow secure the moments that were captured in the images inside the room.

I pad across the hallway. I see her back as soon as I walk over the threshold and into the room. She's wearing the sweater I had on last night. It dips below her ass. Her legs are bare, her hair a mess around her shoulders.

"Noah." Her voice is soft.

I doubt that she heard me approaching. I sense when she's in a room as much as she senses when I'm close. We feel each other's energy. We feed off of it.

"I wanted to show you this last night." I walk up behind her, wrapping my arms around her shoulders. "This is why I keep coming back."

She nods. The movement slight as I rest my chin on the top of her head. "Your mom was so beautiful. I had no idea. You look a lot like her."

Ben looks more like my mom than I do. He was gifted with her long lashes. His jawline has the same curve as hers. I hated him for that after she died. I despised the fact that he could look in the mirror whenever he wanted and see parts of her reflected back at him. I always had to pull out the folded picture I kept in my wallet when I wanted to see my mom's face.

"When was that one taken?" She holds a half empty glass of water in her hand as she gestures towards a framed picture on an easel near the window. "Is that you or Ben with your back to the camera?"

"That's Ben." I hug her. "We were twelve. She was teaching him about roses. She was always teaching us about roses."

"She loved roses." The words aren't a question. She's repeating the fact to herself as if she's going to store it somewhere away inside of her. "What about that one?"

I assume she's talking about the one next to it. "My parents were going to a charity dinner the night I took that. I tried at least ten times to get them both to smile at the same time."

"Neither of them is smiling," she points out.

"I know." I chuckle faintly. "They were arguing about what time the event started. I don't know why. They were never on time for anything."

"That's the day you graduated." Her head tilts to the right. "She was sick then."

It was the only picture that had brought tears to my eyes when I found it in a box in the closet of the spare bedroom here. My brother and I are both dressed in our caps and gowns. I'm smiling brightly as if I don't have a fucking care in the world. Ben is barely able to grin. My mom is sitting between us in a wheelchair. She's frail and thin. The oxygen hose in her nose an everlasting reminder of the day she died.

I'd stared at that picture for hours after I found it. It encapsulated everything that had torn my brother and me apart for years. I'd blamed him for her death, certain that he'd been purposefully negligent when he failed to hook up her oxygen properly the day she died. He made a mistake and when I first saw this picture I realized that her will to live had already disappeared.

The joy in her eyes wasn't there anymore. The color of her skin was ashen and the infection that had brought her to death's door would have pushed her over the threshold if she wouldn't have died the day she did. My mother knew her time was limited. I see that when I look at the way she's clinging to our hands in the picture. She held on so she could watch us graduate from high school.

`   "She looks peaceful." Her left hand jumps up to my forearm. "I think she was happy for you and Ben. She was happy that you were on the cusp of your futures."

"My mom was a lot like you." It's something I've always wanted to say but the words have never made it onto my tongue, and past my lips. Each time I've been ready to say it, I've stopped myself. I always thought it was because I'd break down remembering what a great mother I had. Now I know I've been holding the words inside because it means I'm looking to the future, instead of clinging to the past.

Her breathing slows as she absorbs what I just said. "That's the nicest thing you've ever said to me. All I want is to be a good mom, and a good wife."

"You're a fucking amazing mom, Alexa." I kiss the top of her head. "You're the perfect wife. You're my every dream come true."

I hear the hushed sobs as she tries to hold them inside. I know my wife. I know the tears aren't just from my words. I know she's crying because of what I lost, and what we've gained together. This is why I brought her to Boston with me. I wanted her to see and feel the emotion in these images the same way that I do when I look at them.

"You're going to show these in a gallery, aren't you?" She brings my hand to her lips and kisses the palm. "They're framed like this because you're going to display them."

"That's the plan." My hold on her tightens as I push my chest into her back. "I want the world to see my mom the way I did before I let her go forever."

"I understand." She tilts her head back so she can look up at me. "You never have to completely let her go, Noah. We'll tell the kids about her. We'll show them these pictures. We'll both make certain they know who their grandmother was."

60

It may be the greatest gift she's ever given to me. Alexa's kind understanding is exactly what I need to finally let my mom rest in peace.

CHAPTER 8

"Why are you dressed?" Her eyes rake over the faded jeans and light blue t-shirt I'm wearing. I'd found them in the closet this morning, along with all the other clothes I left behind when I moved to New York.

I'd lived under the assumption that my father had packed everything up and donated it to the shelter a few blocks over when he moved in here last year, but from the looks of it, he's been living out of a suitcase when he is here. Everything is almost exactly where it was when I left.

"You miss my dick already?" I grab the denim material covering my groin. "You need to learn to control yourself, Alexa."

She tightens the belt on the robe she put on after her shower. I recognize it as being one of mine although I doubt I ever wore it. "You're hilarious, Noah."

The stoic expression on her face doesn't match her words. "You're being sarcastic? That's adorable."

A wide grin flashes over her mouth. "Seriously? Why are you dressed? I remember you always being naked when you used to live here."

The house phone rings as if on cue. "It's almost nine. My assistant is prompt. I told her the last time I saw her that we'd be here today and I wanted her to come to meet you."

"You have an assistant?"

I dart my finger in the air as I answer the phone, quietly talking to the doorman of the building. I hear Alexa muttering under her breath.

"Why do you need an assistant?" She's right behind me as I hang up the phone. "What's going on?"

I turn quick on my heel and kiss her softly. "You'll understand the moment you meet her."

She half-shrugs her shoulder as she trudges down the hallway and disappears into the bedroom, where I assume, she'll get dressed.

The faint knock at the door brings an instant smile to my face. I swing the door open with one quick movement. "Opal, I've been waiting for you."

***

"Noah," Alexa whispers my name against my bicep as she clings tightly to my hand. "She's…your assistant…is that what she really is? Noah, she's home…"

I turn quickly and lower my lips to her cheek. "She's proud, Alexa. Opal is a very proud and very talented woman who unfortunately ran into some bad luck."

Her eyes catch mine and I see the instant understanding in her expression. She nods slowly as her thumb slides over my hand.

I had last night all planned out before Alexa and I ended up in bed before nine o'clock. When we left the kids in New York under the care of my dad, I thought we'd have time to talk on the flight to Boston about my work here and Opal. That hadn't happened.

A woman, who has a son enrolled in the school that Alexa teaches at, sat across the aisle from her. The two of them spent the entire flight talking about geometry. Alexa practically gave the woman a primer so she could tutor her son. I admire her commitment to her job, but I wanted her completely focused on my needs this weekend. It's selfish. I feel no guilt about that. Everything I'm doing here in Boston is to be the best man I can possibly be so my wife and my kids are proud of me.

"I'll take your coat." I let go of Alexa's hand as I approach Opal who is standing near the windows looking out at the view of the city. "I didn't have a chance to run out to get any food, but I'll order something in."

Opal nods as I slip the heavy wool coat I bought her last month off her shoulders. "That's kind of you, Noah. I was going to bring up some coffee but I ran out of time."

It's money. She ran out of money. I know that. I pay her a few hundred dollars cash each time I come to Boston to help me organize photos, and clean my office and just talk about life but the woman barely keeps a dollar of that.

I know once she leaves my place she heads straight to the shelter she stays at and hands it over to them. I drop in there from time-to-time now when I want to invite her to spend the day with me. It's where I first met her almost a year ago. She was hunched over a magazine, dated five years ago, reading an article about the benefits of vacationing in St. Tropez.

I took the seat next to her and as her eyes traveled over my face and settled on my scar, she didn't bat an eyelash. She smiled at me. It wasn't one of those forced grins I've grown accustomed to from strangers. It was warm and genuine.

We talked that day about death. Her husband died five years ago leaving her with a mountain of debt and no way to climb out of the financial hole she was in. She had no children to lend a hand or any siblings nearby she could stay with. Her pride held her back from asking her friends for anything. Instead, she scraped by on the minimum wage job she held at a drug store until they gave her two week's severance pay and no notice that her work with them was done.

She ended up at the shelter when the temperature got too cold for her to stay outside. All she owns are the clothes on her back, the pictures of her life, and the papers that document who she is. It's all in a knapsack she keeps strapped to her back.

It wasn't until I stood to leave that day and she reached towards me with her outstretched hand that I knew that she understood me better than most people I've ever met. Her right hand was missing its thumb. The rest of her fingers were a twisted reminder of an accident at a factory she once worked at. Her left hand fared much better, the damage not as severe but she wasn't looking for pity. She didn't need it.

Trying to explain to my wife how I ended up befriending a homeless woman, decades older than me, was never the challenge. Alexa understands I'm far from typical when it comes to the people I choose to get close to. I used to have soul searching discussions with Bernie, the sandwich delivery guy, before Alexa walked into my life.

I don't judge anyone based on their age, or how they look or what's in their wallet. I let people's souls speak to me and Opal's was crying out when I first saw her that day. She needed a friend and so did I.

I wanted my wife here in Boston so she could see what I see in Opal and so she could understand why I need to have my work in the spotlight again. It's not for the accolades, or for the money. It's to feed the creative part of me that has gotten lost beneath the endless hours of editing family photos for other people and the never-ending drive to keep my schedule full.

"I was wondering if I might see those pictures you took last time you were here." Opal points to my camera, which I'd put down on the coffee table after taking a picture of Alexa this morning.

I'd made her sit on the windowsill in my sweater while I got on my knees in front of her and captured her vision forever. She looked more beautiful today than she ever has before. I wanted to save that so I could look at it twenty years from now and remember how I thought I loved her as much as I could when I took the picture, yet knowing that by then, I'll love her even more.

"I have them on a memory card. It's in the other room."

I arch my brows as I glance at Alexa, looking for permission to leave the two of them alone. She's too busy staring at Opal to even notice me.

"Opal, I can make us a coffee." She steps across the room in the direction of the kitchen. "I brought a container of my favorite blend in my bag with me. I remembered that the coffee Noah used to drink here was crap."

Opal laughs loudly, a sound I've rarely heard. "I'd like that, Alexa. I told Noah the last time I saw him that I knew I'd love his wife as much as I love him."

I turn towards the hallway, suddenly feeling like the weight of the world has fallen off my shoulders.

CHAPTER 9

"I'm no expert," she stops herself as her hands slide over my bare chest.

"I disagree." I pull in a slow, deep breath. "After what your mouth just did to my dick, I'd say you're an expert, Alexa. That was fucking amazing."

Her tongue races over her bottom lip. That's the same tongue that popped out of her mouth to show me my release before she swallowed it after blowing me. I adjust her on my lap as I feel my cock hardening again.

"Watch it or I'll be ready to go right away."

"Promises, promises." She inches back on my thighs, her hands resting on my shoulders.

I'd brought her back to the bed after Opal left. We'd spent the entire day with her, sharing lunch and then dinner before Alexa packed up the leftovers for her to take with her. She asked Opal to stay in the spare room, but she was insistent that her friends at the shelter were waiting for her. I'd given her three hundred dollars on the promise that she'd keep at least twenty of that for herself. She'd smiled without agreeing to my terms. She'd pocketed the money, had hugged both Alexa and I and then left the penthouse wrapped in her coat, gloves and hat to face the bitterly cold January air.

I push my back into the headboard, my hands resting on my wife's thighs. "What aren't you an expert at?"

"Photography." Her voice is small, hesitant. "You've taught me a lot about it but I'm not an expert."

"No one needs to be an expert to be a photographer." I laugh. "Have you seen Instagram? Facebook? Anyone with a camera or a phone with a camera is a photographer."

"You haven't spent all this time framing your mom's pictures just because you want to show them to the world."

It's not a question. She's too smart to ask me that. She has way too much insight into the man that I am.

"There's more to it than that, Alexa."

"You miss being the Noah Foster, don't you?" She scratches her chin; the movement causing her breasts to bounce.

I love that she hasn't tried to get beneath the sheet or pull on a robe. She's as completely comfortable nude as I am even though we're talking about something as meaningful as my career.

"I don't miss what I used to do." I don't need to talk about who I used to be. Alexa knew that guy. She fell in love with me despite the fact that I was well known for inviting prostitutes to this apartment to either photograph them or fuck them. "I miss taking pictures that matter to me. I miss expressing myself through my work."

"I saw those pictures you took of Opal," she says delicately. "I looked at your camera. I saw the pictures of her and the others."

73

The others? For some reason those words sound too harsh and empty coming from my wife's lips. I know there's no hidden meaning behind them, but they strike me as detached, or maybe just out-of-place. "The other people who stay at the shelter, you mean?"

"Yes, I'm talking about them." Her fingers trail lazily over a tattoo in the middle of my chest of a cross. I'd gotten it shortly after the twins came to live with us, when we were still fostering them. It held no particular meaning to anyone other than me. My mother had worn a cross around her neck that my father gave to her the day my brother and me were born. The dark tattoo was in honor of her. A symbol of my love for my children, my silent promise to guide them on life's path the best way I know how.

"What about them, Alexa?"

"Why haven't you gotten Opal a place to live?" she asks. "I see why you care about her. She's a very sweet person."

I'm not offended by the question. It's not thoughtless. It's honest.

"I offered, repeatedly. Opal refused."

"We have so much." She pats my stomach. "We have more than enough to eat. We own two homes. We don't have to worry about money."

It's guilt that laces her words. I hear it. She feels it. I do as well. I have since I was a young boy and realized that the condo I lived in was more spacious than the crowded apartments my friends would go home to. I learned to hide the fact that my parents would take Ben and me to Europe during summer break and Aspen for our winter holiday. My mother came from money, a lot of money. I've never wanted for a damn thing my entire life.

"We are generous, Alexa." I squeeze her thighs. "We give a lot."

"I don't think it's enough."

"We can give more," I offer. "We can go to the shelter today and I'll write them a check."

Her lips part and there's a brief moment of silence before she speaks. "I'd like that but there's something else."

"What?"

"I said I'm no expert, Noah," she begins before she stops to point at the doorway. "Go look at your camera. You need to really look at those pictures you took of Opal and the other people at the homeless shelter. Those are the pictures you need to let the world see. There is so much in those faces. I felt so much when I looked at them."

Whatever she may have felt when she studied the images on my camera is in her voice. I hear raw emotion. It's sadness and as I stare into my wife's beautiful blue eyes, I know that she may just have given me the purpose I've been searching for.

CHAPTER 10

"I've been thinking more about a baby." I set a cup of coffee on the table in front of Alexa. "I think we need to get on the same page. I don't like that we're not."

Her fingers trail over her forehead before she snaps her head up to look at my face. "I know that you're happy with things the way they are."

"How could I not be happy with the family we have?" I sit in the chair next to her, pulling her bare feet into my lap. "We have the most amazing son and daughter in the world."

She moans as I push my thumb into the sole of her right foot. "That feels so good. My feet have been so sore."

I smile knowing that she's working herself as hard as she is. She's on her feet all day at school and once she walks through the door of our apartment, she's busy chasing after our twins. She doesn't slow down until she's fast asleep next to me.

"I want to understand why you want a baby, Alexa."

"You know why I want one."

I massage her heel, my fingers roaming over the smooth skin. Is it possible for a woman to have perfect feet? If it is, my wife owns them. "You feel a void inside?"

Since we got to Boston yesterday, I realized something pretty substantial. I've been so preoccupied with trying to fill the hole I feel inside of me that's related to my work that I've been ignoring the same bottomless pit that Alexa feels inside of her.

"I feel like there's something I'm missing." She rests her hand on her chest. "I love being a mom. I wouldn't trade it for anything."

"What is it then?"

She pushes her right foot into my palm, stretching her leg out as she does. "You seriously could do this for money, Noah. Women would pay to have your hands on them."

"I'm not going to respond to that." I chuckle deeply. "You're the only woman I want to touch."

"Do you ever think about what our baby would look like?" Her breath staggers. "If we could have had a baby, do you think it would have had your eyes?"

It's a conversation I always avoid. I've never faulted Alexa for not being able to get pregnant. If I had to choose between her and a child born of my blood and bone, I'd choose her every single time, over and over until I take my last breath.

The irony of my job is that I walk into homes where women confess to me that they weren't even sure they wanted their baby but now that they have him or her, they're grateful. They throw those words out like they mean nothing and as I snap frame after frame of the small faces and tiny hands of their newborn children, I wonder why the universe didn't see fit to give my wife a child of her own.

I mourn for the loss she must feel in the knowledge that she'll never carry her own child in her body. She'll never feel it kicking, or sense its presence. She tells me all the time that she's fine with that but she's not. Her desperate desire to adopt an infant is evidence of that.

Alexa can't have our baby, but she wants a baby. She wants the experience of holding an infant, and swaddling it next to her chest. She wants that baby to only know her as its mother and me as its father.

How in the hell can I take that away from her when she's given me everything?

"Sometimes I think that I want a baby more than anything." Her hand trails over her stomach, across the black sweater she's wearing. "Then there are times when I don't want things to change at all. I love Max and Chloe so much."

I arch my brow, waiting for her to continue, wanting her to share.

"When we got Max and Chloe I knew that they were born to be our children." She smiles brightly. "You could feel that too, right? It was as if they were waiting for the two of us. "

"They were." I graze my hand over her toes. "Those kids were waiting for us."

I met our children when I stumbled on a community daycare program. I volunteered my time to help and in the process I met my twins. It felt like fate at the time. It still does.

"What if there's another child waiting for all of us?" She pushes her foot into my thigh. "What if our family is supposed to be bigger? What if we're not done yet?"

"We can talk to a lawyer about adoption or we can foster another child."

She folds her hands in her lap, her eyes cast down. "I don't want to go out looking for just any child, Noah. I think if our baby is meant to find us, he or she will."

I don't argue. I don't push because the baby she's looking for may never find us. I now realize the hole that my wife feels inside of her may be the child we'll never be able to conceive.

CHAPTER 11

"Grandpa said you used to be a troublemaker."

I turn towards the soft voice of my daughter. Her small hands are resting on my forearm. She's dressed in her pajamas, her dark hair framing her face. I tucked her in bed more than an hour ago after telling her a story about our dog, Rex. My kids love that dog. I do too although I'll never admit it to them.

"You're a troublemaker," I counter as I pick her up and place her in my lap. "You're supposed to be asleep."

"Max is asleep," she offers as if that's the consolation prize. "He always falls asleep before I do."

I snuggle my face into her hair. "Are you not tired?"

"No." She looks up at me. "Did you get hurt because you were a troublemaker, Daddy?"

Her small brown eyes rest on the scar on my cheek. My children have asked about the scar at various times, in very different ways.

In Max's mind I'm a superhero who was injured while saving the world. I've corrected him by telling him that I was trying to save a friend but the bad guy hurt me. He prefers his story and until he's older, I've decided that correcting him is a waste of his time and mine.

Chloe is different. She's the one I catch staring at my face when she thinks I'm not looking. She's also the one who touched it repeatedly one night when we sat together on the sofa watching a cartoon. She didn't ask me about it then, and I never offered an explanation.

Since that day she's tossed out random questions about whether it hurts and why my twin brother, her Uncle Ben, doesn't have one just like it. I've answered each question with thoughtful tenderness.

I know one day I'm going to have to explain to both of them that I was stabbed when I was trying to fend off the boyfriend of the woman I thought I loved. I'm also going to have to tell them that it cost him his life so I could save hers and mine.

"I know someone hurt you, Daddy." She reaches up to wrap her arm around my shoulder. "I'm sorry that they did that to you."

"Me too."

Her lips skirt over the scar. "If I could kiss it better, I would. I would take it away so it wouldn't hurt you anymore."

There's no way in hell I'm going to get through this without crying. I don't even try and stop the tears. "It doesn't hurt anymore, Princess."

"I think it does."

"Why do you think that?"

Her hand picks up mine and rests it against my cheek, over the scar. "You're sad sometimes. I see you holding your face like this. You look so sad, Daddy."

"I'm not sad." I pull my hand away, cradling hers in mine. "I think about how I got the scar sometimes. That does make me sad."

"I know someone cut you." She tilts her head slightly to the left, her eyes glued to my cheek. "A boy in our class cut his finger with a knife. It looked like that."

I cast my eyes down. "A man cut me with a knife."

Her small hand jumps to my chin and as she tilts my head up to meet her gaze, I see the tears in her own eyes. "I would have stopped him, Daddy. I would have screamed at him until he stopped. I promise I would have saved you."

I pull her into me then, her head resting against my chest as my heart thumps a fast beat. I hold tight to her, wishing I could change my past, but knowing that nothing I can do will ever erase that night from my mind or my face.

***

"You're going to miss me like crazy, aren't you?" I whisper the question into the sweet smelling skin at the back of my wife's neck. She had been fast asleep when I got to bed last night after taking Chloe back into her room and waiting for her to fall asleep.

I didn't wake her when I got up an hour ago and showered, dressed and gave the kids their breakfast.

"Not really," she says sleepily. "You hog the blankets, Noah. You're like a fucking giant. You take up most of the bed."

I chuckle deeply. "You're the blanket hog, Alexa. When I got in bed last night, you had them wrapped tightly around you. I was freezing cold the entire night."

"I'm naked."

"What?" I yank at the edge of the blanket, trying desperately to find a way in but she's encased herself. "Let me see. I don't believe you."

"Like I'm going to lie about that." she moves her head slightly. "Aren't you supposed to be on your way to the airport by now?"

I am. I'm catching a flight to Boston in less than two hours to meet my brother. That means I should already be out the door and on my way. "I want to see your body, Alexa."

"It hasn't changed since yesterday." She kicks her feet slightly, the motion doing nothing to dislodge her from the blankets. "You can see me when you get home tomorrow."

Why the fuck does that feel like forever right now. "We have time now. I can fuck you quickly. I can do it in the next five and still make my flight."

"What horny girl can refuse an offer like that? A fast fuck on the Noah Foster's cock?"

"It's not happening, is it?" I try to sound deflated but she's way too cute right now. "Can I at least get a kiss goodbye?"

She moves swiftly, kicking the blankets free, revealing a pair of jeans and the same god awful ugly sweater she was wearing when we went to Boston together last week. "Diana should be walking through the door any second and I already called an Uber. He's waiting downstairs for us. I'll go with you and kiss you goodbye before you go through security."

"Cock tease." I laugh as I graze my lips over hers.

"Only for you." She giggles. "Only for you."

CHAPTER 12

"Dad might show up," Ben says as he slides out of the backseat of the taxi when I greet him on the street in front of my building in Boston. "I spoke to him this morning."

I pull my brother into a hug. A few years ago I thought we'd never speak again. Now, I can't go a day without talking to him or texting him. He's my best friend.

"I talked to him too." I reach for his overnight bag. "He's flying in from San Antonio later today. He'll crash here tonight."

"It'll be good to see him."

I look up at the sky. The looming clouds hold a promise of the snowstorm that the news outlets have been talking about all day. I ran down to the street in just a t-shirt and jeans when Ben called to say he was almost here. "Let's go inside. I'm freezing. Hopefully dad lands before the storm hits."

"I hope so. I haven't seen him in a few weeks." He falls in step behind me as we enter the lobby. "Whenever he's in Manhattan he's been working with Max on a secret project for your birthday."

I stop in place and turn on my heel. "You just blew that surprise, dude."

He chuckles deeply. "I didn't. Wait until you see what it is."

I want to push but I'm not about to steal anything away from my son. I start walking towards the elevator again. "It's your birthday too that day."

"I'll be there for the unveiling."

I stop, once again turning to look at him. "Shut up about the surprise. You're fucking this up."

"I'm not." He taps his hand on my shoulder. "I hope one day I get to have a son like Max. He idolizes you."

"He's a great kid."

"Have you figured out what we're going to do today?" He slides his dress shoe across the marble floor as we wait for the elevator. "We can go to mom's grave."

"She wouldn't want that." I motion for him to step into the lift once the doors open. "I have something else in mind."

"Alright." He shrugs his shoulders. "I'm going to defer to you since you're the oldest."

I laugh. "Don't you forget that, Doc. Never forget that."

***

"I've tried to tell Kayla about how beautiful mom was." He skims his hand over her face in the image he's standing in front of. "I need to show her this picture. This says it all."

It does. It's a picture that I can't take credit for. My dad took it the day we were born. He actually took three pictures. One is of my mother holding both of us, one in each of her arms. The other is of her holding me and this one, the one I framed for Ben, is our mother cradling him when he's only a few hours old.

"I want you to take that home."

He turns towards me, his eyes locking on mine. "This is for me? You framed it for me?"

"I thought we should each have one." I nod towards a similar one on my desk. "That's me and mom."

He crosses the floor and looks down at the framed picture. "We looked almost identical the day we were born. We don't look as much alike now."

"You wish you looked like me," I joke. "We both know I'm the better looking one."

He hesitates only briefly. "My wife would argue that point with you. She tells me I'm hot."

"She has to say that, she's married to you."

He shakes his head as he chuckles. "I heard about the photo exhibit from Kayla. You're showing these pictures of mom?"

I scan the office. All the images of our mother are still in the same place they were last week when Alexa and I were here. I didn't move them when I arrived at the penthouse this morning even though that was my intention.

I've spent the past week trying to decide how to best utilize the gallery space I've been offered next month. "Alexa had a different suggestion. I might go that way."

He rests the picture in his hands on the desk. "What way is that?"

"I'll show you." I move across the room to a filing cabinet. "I made a few prints in New York and brought them with me. I want your opinion. I want dad to see them too."

I rifle through the large envelope I carried on the airplane with me. I had studied the pictures on the flight here and with each mile that passed I was more convinced that this is what I need to share if I'm going to put my work in front of the public again.

"I've been thinking a lot about how private mom was." I don't turn to look at him as I continue, "I can't ask her for permission to display these pictures but I can honor her in another way."

"What way?" He's behind me now. I can tell by the tone of his voice.

"Remember when mom would take us to the grocery store?" I pick out two pictures and hold them in my hand as I turn. "We'd buy a bunch of stuff for the food drive."

His eyes drop to my hands. "We'd stop there on our way home. She'd make us unload all the food. We even had to go back sometimes on Saturday mornings to help the staff sort through stuff."

"She used to tell us we got to help," I tell him. "She would correct me when I said we had to do it. She'd tell me got to because we were lucky."

"I remember."

I flip the pictures in my hands over so they're visible to my brother. "I started donating at the shelter that's three blocks over a couple of years ago. Whenever I was back here, I'd stop in there."

He reaches for the pictures, tugging on them. "You took these when you were there?"

I nod. "The people there aren't looking for handouts. They're hard-working. They want to contribute."

His eyes scan the photographs, stopping on the one of Opal. "This woman is beautiful."

"That's Opal," I say clearly. "She comes here to help me sometimes."

"This is the Opal that Alexa told Kayla about?"

My wife can barely contain herself when it comes to sharing news about any aspect of her life. I don't fault her for telling her best friend about Opal.

"Mom would have preferred if I made a show of these." I tap the edge of Opal's picture. "I'll take more. I'll capture their experience. I'll share it with others."

He nods slowly. "Mom would be proud of you. She'd be so proud of you for doing this."

'You're a doctor, Ben." I pat his shoulder. "She would have told every single person she met that her son was a doctor."

He meets my gaze. "I wish she was here. I miss her more now, you know?"

"I know. I know exactly how you feel."

CHAPTER 13

"His flight is delayed but he's going to be here tonight." I glide the full bottle of beer across the table towards Ben. "We'll walk back to the penthouse and meet him there."

"Do you think he's happy?"

"Dad?" I pick up a fry and pop it in my mouth. "He seems happy enough to me."

He takes a swallow of the beer. "I think about losing Kayla sometimes. I don't know how he did it. How do you go on after something like that?"

I thought about the same thing once too. I imagined what my life would be like if Alexa died. I couldn't actually focus on the idea of it because of the instant panic that set in. I'd go on for the kids. I'd make sure they healed and grew into the people she wants them to be, but I'd be dead inside. I'd be empty without her.

"He's a strong man," I offer. "He's dealt with way too much shit in his life."

He drinks more beer, gulps it actually. "I thought he hated me for years. I know he couldn't look at me without thinking about mom's death."

I'm not going to sugar coat it to shield him from the truth. We've talked this out with our dad, Ron. The three of us sat in a bar one night and let loose. "He was heartbroken. We all were after she died."

"I talked to the doctor who was taking care of her a couple of months ago." His eyes close briefly. "I was here at a conference. He was there too. He actually remembered her case."

Medical jargon is a foreign language to me. I went in to see Ben at the hospital when I had a sore throat last fall and he tossed out some term that sounded like an Italian dish. It was an infection, cured within days with a round of antibiotics. "Tell me in English what he said."

He smiles. "They told her before she left the hospital that she had weeks left to live. I fucked up when I messed up her oxygen that day but her time was limited. We would have lost her before the end of that summer."

I knew it. I might not have recognized it when I was eighteen and mourning the loss of every single minute I could have had with her. "She had a virus? Dad said that's what it was."

He studies my face carefully. "I was going to talk to dad about this first. I wanted to tell him that I know, before I told you, but he shuts me down whenever I try and bring it up."

"Dad's not here." I wave my arm over the table. "Tell me. I have a right to know."

"She had late stage breast cancer. It had spread…everywhere. She avoided doctors for years and when she finally went in because she couldn't stop vomiting they told her she had a stomach virus and that she had terminal cancer."

"Cancer," I repeat the word back. "Why didn't dad tell us that?"

"She probably told him not to. We were graduating, Noah." He picks up the bottle of beer but doesn't bring it to his mouth. "You know mom. She protected us from everything. That's who she was."

"She did protect us." I heave a sigh knowing that keeping those pictures of her private so they can remain treasures to our family is the right thing to do. I need to protect her memory. "She was a fighter, Ben. She was the definition of a fighter."

"Here's to mom." He holds his beer in the air between us. "Happy Birthday, Mom."

I raise my bottle and clink it against his. "Happy Birthday, Mom. I love you."

***

"Where's Opal?" I ask one of the residents of the shelter that I photographed a few months ago. "I don't see her."

He looks around, his eyes stopping on the small, gathered groups of people. "She was here this morning. I haven't seen her since."

"What does that mean?" I pat him on the shoulder to stall him as he starts to walk away. "It's snowing outside. The temperature is freezing. She has to be here."

"Nope." He points to her knapsack sitting on the edge of a cot. "That's her bag there but she's not here. She told me to watch it when she went for a walk."

I look at Ben but his eyes are glued to his phone. After we left the restaurant, I suggested we stop at the shelter so I could introduce him to Opal. My plan is to offer her an actual full-time job caretaking at my penthouse.

I'm going to sell eventually but for now, I'll keep the place and work on my photography project when I'm in town. Opal can help me organize. She'll earn a paycheck from me and I'll have the help I need. It's a win-win. It's fucking brilliant and best of all it will get her out of the shelter and give her a chance to get back on her feet. It's a small step but she's been good to me and I want to repay that.

As for our dad, Ben already offered his empty condo here if he needs a place to stay when he's in town. He's a nomad now so who knows where he'll be a week from now.

"What's wrong?" Ben taps my shoulder. "Is she not around?"

"That's her stuff." I walk over to pick up the knapsack. "This is everything she owns, Ben. She wouldn't just walk away and leave it here."

"It's brutal outside, Noah." He points to the window. The steady stream of snow falling makes it impossible to see beyond a foot or two. "She's probably at another facility. We can check on some of the close ones."

I wouldn't know how to do that. I shouldn't be this worried about her. She can take care of herself. I know that but she's become a friend. She's important to me now. I can't explain it, but I feel a connection to her. I always have.

"Are you two boys looking for Opal?" A female voice pulls both of our attention to the left as her hand reaches out to touch Ben's chest. "I've seen you here before, but you're new."

Ben's eyebrows pop up as the older woman gropes him through his coat. "My brother is friends with Opal. We'd like to talk to her."

"She went down to that park she likes this morning."

"This morning? She hasn't come back since?"

"I'm not her babysitter." She leans in close to Ben. "I'd babysit you though. I'd even do it for free."

"We're leaving." I pull on his arm. "We're going to find Opal."

CHAPTER 14

"You're sure this is the park she would go to?" Ben calls from across the vacant park towards me. I can't see him. I can't see shit because it's snowing so fucking hard right now.

"This is it," I yell back. "I walked her here one day. She used to come here with her husband."

The lamp posts that dot the landscape aren't throwing enough light for me to see anything. There's no way in hell she's here. She would have sought shelter somewhere. That makes the most sense. What makes no sense at all is that the shelter she lives in is less than two blocks away.

"I called every hospital, Noah." Ben is right in front of me now, snow peppering his dark hair and his coat. "She hasn't been admitted. There are no Jane Does either. She has to be safe somewhere."

"Where?" I bark the question back at him as I scrub my hand over my forehead. "I'm sorry. I'm worried, Ben. She wouldn't leave this shit behind."

His eyes fall to the knapsack I'm still clinging to. "You said that her and her late husband had friends. She might have met up with one of them and decided to spend the night."

It makes sense. It's definitely plausible.

"I wish to fuck she would have taken me up on my offer to get her a phone," I say it aloud. "I wouldn't have to worry so much if I could call her."

"Let's head back to the shelter." He pulls the collar of his coat closer to his neck. "The temperature is dropping fast. We're too exposed. We need to get inside too."

I know he's right. We should try and find a taxi and head back to the shelter so I can leave her things there for when she shows back up. If we do that, we can be back at the penthouse, having a brandy with our dad, within the hour.

My brother taps his hand on my chest before he points to the street in the distance. I can barely make out the passing traffic. "Let's head back up that way. I'll lead the way."

I nod as I watch him take a step forward and that's when I see it. It's the faintest movement in the distance. It's the only flash of darkness against the white snow but since it's directly under a lamp post, it's unmistakable.

"She's there." I grab Ben's shoulder as I run past him. "Opal's on that bench."

***

I kneel in the snow next to her. Her eyes are closed, her breathing slow. It's so fucking slow that my brother, the doctor, is straining to hear it.

"Call an ambulance now, Noah," he repeats. "Now."

"She's going to die," I say as I fish in my pocket for my phone. "You're not going to let her die, Ben. You tell me that right now."

He ignores me completely as he pushes his coat from his shoulders, draping it over her. "Take your coat off. Put it on her now. We have to warm her up."

I yell into the phone, trying to get the 911 operator to understand the address of the park. I say it over and over again, stressing how important it is that they get their fucking asses here now.

Ben tugs the phone away from me. He speaks into it quickly, talking about her heart, her core temperature, breathing, not breathing, he tells them to hurry.

He yanks the zipper of my jacket down, pulling the coat off of me in one quick movement. He places it over her.

"Don't touch her." He pushes my hands away as I reach to grab hers. She's wearing those shitty thin gloves that she always is. Her hands must be freezing. They have to be cold as ice.

"You can't just touch her, Noah. She may go into shock. We have to get her inside. We have to get her to the hospital."

The sound of the sirens approaching turns him around. "You go get them. Tell them where we are."

I don't hesitate. I race through the park, running as fast as my legs will take me. I fall twice in the snow as I lose my balance but I get up, my stride barely breaking as I wave my bare arms in the air towards the ambulance as it pulls up next to the curb.

CHAPTER 15

"Thirty minutes more and she wouldn't have survived." Ben speaks softly into his phone. "They're not sure yet. She hasn't woken up. Her vitals are stabilizing but it's too soon to know how long she was exposcd."

I turn away from where he's sitting. I finished my call with Alexa too quickly. I had to say goodbye when I started to cry. I didn't want her to hear my voice breaking. It kills her when I'm upset. She wants to comfort me. I need that too and that can't happen when she's in New York with our kids and I'm here.

"Give Emerson a kiss for me. I'll be on the first available flight out tomorrow," he pauses. "I'll tell him. I love you too, Kayla."

He ends the call before he walks over to the nurse's desk. I hear the murmur of his voice mixed with that of a woman.

"You can go in and see her, Noah."
He gestures towards a long corridor. "I'll
go with you if you want."

I reach up to his outstretched hand.
I grab hold of it, allowing him to pull me
back up to my feet from the chair I fell into
when we arrived at the ER. "What did the
nurse say?"

"Nothing." He rests both his hands
on my shoulders. "Kayla wanted me to tell
you that she's praying for Opal though.
How did you know she was on that bench?
I didn't see her when I walked past it."

"She moved her arm, or her leg." I
shrug. "Something caught my eye. I knew
it had to be her."

"Once she's awake they'll be able to
determine if something else is wrong."

"Something else?" I take a step
back. "She almost froze to death, Ben.
That's what's wrong with her."

His expression softens. I don't see this side of my brother very often. I don't want to see it. It's the doctor side that's about to deliver bad news. "There has to be a reason why she was on that bench, Noah. If she was fine, she would have gotten up and walked back to the shelter before the storm hit."

Of course he's fucking right. I know that.

"One step at a time." His hand darts to my back. "Let's go see her and we'll go from there."

***

"What the fuck is wrong with people?"

I'm asking that question, but it's strictly rhetorical.

"I'm not sure what I can tell you about that." The nurse perks up. "When you work in a hospital there's a lot wrong with people."

Ben's brow pops up as he nods towards the nurse. "She knows what she's talking about, Noah."

"You must be Ben."

We turn in unison at the sound of Opal's voice as her eyes flutter open.

"You look exactly like your brother," she says quietly. "He told me you two weren't identical twins."

"We're not." I take a step closer to the bed. "We're fraternal twins."

"I'd know he was your brother in an instant." She pats the bed next to her. "I'm not in the hospital, am I?"

I stand above her looking down at her face. The color is starting to come back in her cheeks. The prognosis the doctor shared with Ben twenty minutes ago is good.

"Did you fall Opal? You fell at the park, didn't you?"

Her right hand darts to her forehead. "I remember crashing down on a patch of ice near a bench. I think I cracked my head."

"You broke your hip." I gesture towards her legs. "You must have been in so much pain."

"I remember that now." She stares at my face. "I sat on the bench to rest. It hurt to walk. I asked a young woman to help but she didn't hear me."

"How do people just walk past that?" I ask Ben as much as I ask myself. "When did we stop caring? I don't understand."

"This is a private room, isn't it?" Opal tries to lean forward but the discomfort pushes her back into place. The pained expression on her face is evidence of that. "I can't afford this. I don't know what coverage I have but it's not going to cover this."

"Everything is covered." Ben walks to the other side of the bed. "You'll be well taken care of here, Opal."

"You're as nice as Noah said you were." She reaches for my hand. "He told me his brother was a doctor."

"That I am." His eyes fall to her hands for just a moment. "Noah told me you've been a good friend to him. He didn't tell me you were beautiful too."

That brings a blush to her cheeks. "If I would have known that breaking my hip would bring two handsome men to my bedside, I might have tried that trick years ago."

CHAPTER 16

The door of Opal's hospital room opens slightly before my dad's face pops into view.

"Noah? Ben? Which one of you is hurt?"

Opal's brow furrows at the intrusion but she doesn't say a thing.

"Dad." I move across the room quickly, not sure if I should stop him from walking into the room or not. Opal is decent. She's covered in layers of blankets and a hospital gown but she's just been through a hellish experience. I doubt she wants a room full of strangers watching her as she's trying to rest.

"We're both fine. We can talk out in the hallway."

"Who is this?" My dad ignores my words and brushes right past me. "Someone tell me what's going on. I got a text from Ben saying you two had an emergency and he was in an ambulance on his way here."

Ben turns to our dad. "I was riding along, dad. Noah's friend fell in a park. She hurt herself."

My dad stops as he reaches the foot of Opal's bed. His eyes graze over her face.

"Are you okay? Did my sons rescue you?" It's a lighthearted joke that actually brings a smile to Opal's face.

She smooths her hand over her short blonde hair. "They saved my life. You should be proud of your sons."

"I am." He looks at me, then Ben. "My boys both make me very proud."

"We should go." Ben reaches for my dad's elbow. "We've already been here too long."

My dad doesn't move. He just stares. He fucking stares at Opal's face and I realize that it's still my mom's birthday and this woman has to be the same age as her. He's thinking about that. He has to be thinking about mom.

He pushes Ben's hand away as he rounds the bed until he's standing right next to Opal.

She looks up at him, the corners of her lips pulling up into a smile.

"Dad, let's go." Ben's voice is more insistent but my dad ignores it.

"You're sure you're okay? Do you need anything?"

Opal reaches out towards my father with her right hand and he doesn't hesitate as he pulls it into his.

"It's you. It's you, Ronnie, isn't it?"

"Opal?" He brings her hand to his lips. "I can't believe it's you."

"You remember me?"

"I told you I'd never forget you, didn't I?" He leans down and brushes his lips over her forehead.

I look at Ben. He looks at me.

"Is someone going to tell me what's going on?" The nurse effectively breaks the moment when she walks back into the room. "Patients are only allowed two visitors at a time."

"I'm not leaving." My dad sits on the edge of the bed next to Opal. "This here is Opal. She was my very first kiss. My very first love."

"What?" That's all I manage to get out.

"You and Opal know each other?" Ben asks. "You two actually know each other?"

"Opal sat next to me in first grade." He wipes a tear from her cheek. "I passed her notes. I told her I loved her. I gave her a Valentine's Day card I made myself. The very first one I ever gave to anyone."

"I have it." Her voice is soft. "I kept it, Ronnie."

"You don't have that still." He leans forward to look into her eyes. "That was more than fifty years ago now."

"My bag, Noah. I saw it here." Opal's voice is calm. "Can you get it for me?"

I've stepped into some dream. There is no fucking way this is real.

I hand the knapsack to my father and he hands it to Opal.

"Open it, Ronnie. It's in there somewhere."

He does. He pulls out a few pieces of clothing, some folded papers, dozens of photographs and greeting cards, a worn passport and then as his hand dives back into the bag one last time, he stops. He stops because he knows.

Ben knows.

I fucking know too.

"You kept it, Opal." He pulls out a faded red piece of paper. "You kept this for all those years."

I step closer to get a better look. I have to. I should actually be recording this with my phone because there's no fucking way Alexa is ever going to believe this.

"Roses are red," my dad starts reading the handwritten words he wrote when he was a child on the card. "Violets are blue. You like me and you know I like you."

Opal nods. "Read the signature."

"Love," my dad's voice cracks. "Love, Ronnie Foster."

CHAPTER 17

"Your dad is the most romantic man in the world, Noah," Alexa whispers those words into my neck.

"I just fucked you. I don't want to hear about how romantic my old man is right now."

She buries her face in my shoulder to quiet her laughter.

"He was six-years-old when he gave Opal that card." I point out as I run my fingers along her bare shoulder. "That wasn't romance. It's puppy love."

"Puppy love?" She's on her elbows, her chin resting in her hands. "She kept that card with her forever because she still loved him. That's not puppy love, Noah."

I know it's not. I've seen Opal and my dad together at least four times since she fell and broke her hip. They're living together in my place in Boston. I told him I'd hire a nurse to care for her after her surgery, but he wouldn't hear of it. He's been tending to every single one of her needs since that night he walked into her hospital room.

They love each other. They might have been pulled apart when they were twelve-years-old because her family moved to Europe for six years, but whatever bond was forged between them when they were kids, is stronger than ever now.

Each of them tried to find the other when they were widowed but somehow they never crossed paths. I could have made that easier if I would have told her my surname when we met. I never did because I didn't want that sweet older woman to judge me based on all the nude photographs I took. Maybe that was part of their fate and they were destined to find each other again now, when they are both healed and strong enough to love again.

I don't care how it works or why life goes the way it does. I care about my dad's happiness and I haven't seen him this filled with joy in years.

"Ron thought it would be nice if we all went to Boston for your birthday." She lightly kisses my cheek. "Your exhibit opens the day after so we can celebrate one night with the kids and then celebrate the opening the next night with Ben and Kayla."

"I love that plan." I tug her closer to me. "I'm proud of that exhibit, Alexa."

"I'm proud of you," she counters. "When people see those pictures, Noah they're going to be as touched by them as I am."

I'd looked to not only Alexa, but my father and Opal to help me choose which photographs I'll exhibit at the small gallery in Boston. Each is a portrait of someone who has lived at the shelter. Some have gone on to find jobs, others are still there, taking life one day at a time.

Every single person I photographed understood why I wanted to take their picture and where the proceeds of any sales would go to. Each dollar goes into the shelter's coffers.

"Life doesn't get much better than this." I wrap my arms around my wife, pulling her nude body closer to me. "I can't imagine it ever getting better than it is right now."

***

"These are fantastic, Noah." Nicholas Wolf looks down at the headshots I handed him. "You made me look better in these than I do in real life.

"That's the magic of filters," I joke. "I sent a set to your publisher this morning but I wanted to drop these off in person so I could thank you."

"Thank me?" He tucks the photographs back into the envelope. "I should be thanking you for making me look so good."

I can't tell if he's being genuine or not. He's wearing eyeglasses today and looks like he hasn't pulled a comb through his hair in a week. I'm pretty sure he could still walk outside and get laid within three minutes flat.

"You reminded me that I need to keep everything in perspective."

He turns to look right at me, pushing the glasses up and into his hair. "I admire guys like you. You've got it all figured out."

"How so?"

"You have a career that works for you. You're married. You've got kids." His eyes drift to the portrait of the nude woman I took years ago. "How did you find a real woman?"

"A real woman?"

"How did you know your wife wasn't after your money, or just wanted you because of who you are?"

"My wife," I begin with a deep chuckle. "My wife Alexa did not give one fuck about who I was when we met. She had no idea who I was."

"Where was she hiding? Under a rock?"

I laugh loudly this time. "My work didn't interest her. She treated me differently than any other woman ever had before. She never cared about the money, or the fame. She only cared about me."

"Where the hell do I find a woman like that?" he hesitates briefly. "I don't think a woman like that exists in New York."

"My wife walked right through the front door of my apartment," I say. "You never know where your future is. Keep your eyes open, Nick. Keep them wide open."

CHAPTER 18

"Close your eyes, Daddy." Chloe taps her hand on my knee. "Keep them closed until we say you can open them."

I'm trying. I'm trying so fucking hard to be the good dad and to follow the rules. When we got to Boston earlier today, I'd taken my kids to see where I'd gone to school. I treated them to lunch at the same burger place my folks took me to when I was their age and I promised to sit in my home office while they readied the main room for their big birthday surprise.

I haven't even had a chance to say hi to my brother, his wife and their daughter when they arrived. I've been sequestered away from the rest of my family and now, that I've finally been set free, I still have to keep my eyes closed so I don't ruin the surprise my son has been working on for weeks.

What happened to the days when I used to get plastered and pass out on my bedroom floor on my birthday?

"I love you, Daddy."

I almost choke up right there at those whispered words in my ear. That's my guy. That's my little boy telling me how much he loves me. That's enough of a gift to last me through every birthday I'll ever have a chance to celebrate.

"I love you, Daddy."

It's Chloe in my other ear. I press the palms of my hands into my eye sockets trying to ward off the approaching tears. There can't be another man walking the face of this earth who is as lucky as I am.

"Open your eyes, Noah." There is no mistaking that's my beautiful wife's voice.

I do.

I feel the weight of something in my lap so my eyes fall there instinctively. It's a photo album. The exterior may have been plain at one point, but it's not now. It's been decorated with crayons and scribbles and words of adoration from my children.

I study it carefully, reading the words.

Our daddy.

Our hero.

The best pancake maker ever.

He tells the funniest stories.

He gives the best hugs.

He keeps us safe.

"Open it." Max taps my knee. "I can't take it. Just open it."

I look up into his perfect little face. It's lit up with excitement.

"I'll open it," I say quietly.

I do.

The first page is a picture. It's a drawing signed by Max.

"This is me and this is Chloe." His fingers skim across the page. "This is you when you came to the community center the first time. See how happy Chloe and I are."

I nod as I push out a heavy breath.

I turn the page slowly. This time it's a picture of Alexa and me. It was taken just weeks after I met her. My father must have taken it at my gallery showing. Neither of us is looking at the camera, but Alexa is standing in front of me, my arms draped around her.

I know the instant when this was taken. I was explaining a photograph to her. I was telling her how beautiful she is, how she's different from every other woman I've ever known

I dart my eyes up to meet hers and she smiles. She knows. She remembers.

"This is when mommy fell in love with you." Max blushes. "She told us it was then."

"I fell in love with mommy then too."

Our wedding pictures take up the next six pages. Images of the twins as they walked down the aisle and Alexa and I sharing our first dance.

Our honeymoon in Hawaii covers the next two pages. Max with his feet in the ocean, Chloe perched high on my shoulders. A rock we found on the beach is taped to the top of the page and a dried flower that my daughter had worn in her hair the entire time we were there is glued beneath one of the pictures.

I turn each page to uncover a new treasure.

A drawing by Chloe of our first Halloween together, a poem written by Max for Father's Day.

There are pictures of Rex, and of Ben and his family.

There's one of my dad holding the twins on his lap.

My eyes blur more with tears with each page I turn.

I stop when I reach the first empty page halfway through the album.

"This is the end." Max closes the book slowly. "I'll keep filling the book until I'm as old as you are, Daddy. I'll always put something in our book for you."

I pull him into my lap with one arm, the other scooping up Chloe. I cling to them both as my family sings Happy Birthday to my twin brother and me.

Alexa leans down to kiss my cheek as I close my eyes soaking in this moment, this life and every single gift that I've been given.

EPILOGUE

Six Months Later

I walk into the kitchen as soon as I'm home. I see her immediately. She's quietly sitting at the table alone. The warm light from the late afternoon sun bathes her in a glow. Her head is bowed towards her notebook, her brown hair falling in waves around her shoulders.

"Hey sweetie." I stop to kiss the top of her head before I head to the sink to get a glass of water. "How was your day at school?"

"Hi." Her eyes stay buried in the work she's doing. A pencil in her left hand jotting things down. "I had a good day, Noah."

"Noah? Really? You're going to call me Noah now?"

"It's your name," she counters. "I've heard you call grandpa Ron before."

"That's different, Chloe." I sit across from her. "Your grandpa and I used to work together. He's helping me again now with a few things. I call him Ron strictly for business purposes."

"You and I are going to work together one day too, Noah," she says it stoically. "I'm going to be a photographer."

"You are?" I temper my excitement because I know my daughter. Last week she was going to be a veterinarian specializing in hamster care. The week before that her true calling in life was to make glazed donuts.

"Yes." She scribbles something in her notepad. "You can teach me everything you know."

"I can do that."

"When is grandpa and grandma Opal coming back from their honeymoon?" Max walks into the room. "I need to talk to grandpa about my science project."

"Next week." I hand him an apple from the bowl on the table. "I can help with your science project."

"Sorry, Daddy." He pats my shoulder. "This is a grandpa thing. He gets it."

"What does he get?" I ask quickly.

"That's why Max needs grandpa to help him, Noah." Chloe giggles. "If you have to ask about getting it, you're not getting it."

I rub my hands over my face. "Where's mom?"

"She's in the bedroom." Max sits next to me. "Or she might be in your office. She said she had some work to do before you got home."

My beautiful wife is still as devoted to her students as ever. She's trained herself to be on a better schedule though. As soon as she's home from school, she's in the office, grading the work that needs her attention. She's found her balance.

"I'm going to go find her."

"Noah means he's going to go kiss her." Chloe taps the pencil against Max's arm. "We need to stay in here. He's going to tell us that."

"You need to drop the Noah thing, princess." I swipe my fingers through her hair softly. "No calling me that until you actually work with me when you're a grown-up, deal?"

131

Her lips twist into a wide grin. "That's a deal, Daddy. I am going to be a photographer. I want to work with you. I want to be like you."

"I'm going to be a teacher," Max offers as he takes a bite of a pear. "I'll work with mommy. I'll be the principal at her school."

I laugh as I kiss his forehead before I leave the kitchen in search of Alexa.

***

It's one of the first times since we've been together that she doesn't instantly turn as soon as I walk into the office.

I expect to see her at the desk, the red pen in her hand furiously jotting notes on the papers. That's not what I find. She's on her feet, moving quickly from one side of the room to the other as she rearranges a set of framed photographs on a series of nails we've hung in the wall.

"Maybe this one isn't right," she mumbles under her breath. "Noah would like that one better. I do too. It's definitely much better."

She steps back as her hands dart to her hips. Her head tilts to the left. She's restless. She doesn't stand in place for long before she's moving images around again.

"You're choosing what we're going to show here, in New York, at the end of the year?"

My voice startles her. The muted curse words that fall from her lips are evidence of that.

"You scared me shitless, Noah." She turns on her heel. "When did you get home?"

I walk to where she's standing so I can pull her into my arms. I made love to her this morning when we woke, but I've been aching to touch her since then. That's because her scent has been on my face, on my hands and on my body all day.

"I just got here." I kiss her softly. "I've missed you like crazy today."

"You say that every single day."

"It's because I miss you every single day, Alexa."

She circles my waist with her arms, resting her cheek against my chest. "I'm so proud of this exhibit, Noah. You're going to win another award when this opens. I know you are."

She led the standing ovation when I was given an award two months ago from one of the most prestigious photography councils in the country for my work on the Boston exhibit. It was a stellar moment in my career. I was recognized for the series of photographs I'd shown of the people who were living at the shelter. Since then, we've raised hundreds of thousands of dollars to help them.

Venturing out into the streets of New York to capture the folks living with a struggle here, was the next obvious step. It was all because of Alexa. She spearheaded the campaign. She contacted the gallery that we'll be exhibiting in and she's been beside me every weekend when we've gone out to speak with people and take their photographs.

Her passion for this surpasses mine at times. It's become as important to her as it is to me. I still go out and take family portraits, and do professional head shots. My wife teaches her students with the same commitment to learning as she always has but there's more to our experience together now.

This project is our legacy. It's something we are using to teach our children about the value of every person's experience.

"You're doing a great job, Alexa." I gesture towards the row of photographs she's hung on the wall. "You picked the ones I would have chosen."

"Really?" she asks. "You're serious, Noah? You would have picked the same ones?"

"Absolutely," I say with no reservation at all. "Your eye is fucking amazing. You see what I see in these pictures. I know you do."

She nods as she rests her head against me. "I see hope. Every one of these pictures says hope to me. Hope that things will change. Hope that the future will be different."

135

I once thought our future might be different. Alexa's desire to have a baby quieted when she started helping me more. A few weeks ago we sat down and had a brutally honest conversation about our family.

That void within her is gone now. She loves our family exactly as we are, just as I do.

Our lives are full. We have our children, our work, this project and most importantly, my wife and I have each other, today, tomorrow and always.

THANK YOU

Thank you for purchasing my book. I can't even begin to put to words what it means to me. If you enjoyed it, please remember to write a review for it. Let me know your thoughts! I want to keep my readers happy.

For more information on new series and standalones, please visit my website, **www.deborahbladon.com**. There are book trailers and other goodies to check out.

If you want to chat with me personally, please LIKE my page on Facebook. I love connecting with all of my readers because without you, none of this would be possible.

www.facebook.com/authordeborahbladon

Thank you, for everything.

Preview of TORN The Standalone

Featuring Asher Foster

"Are they low enough?"

"Pull them up." I wave my arm in the air towards one of the three female assistants he walked in with. "I need them higher."

He pushes their eager hands away as he adjusts the waistband of his button-fly jeans. I'd told him to strip down to just his pants as soon as he stepped foot into my studio. He had done that effortlessly. His hands tugging the white sweater he was wearing over his head to reveal a toned chest and stomach covered by the expected tattoos.

I'd walked closer to ask him to remove the bracelets and necklaces he had on. His eyes had been glued to mine the entire time.

I admit he's much more attractive than most of the men who traipse through here. His hair may be a tousled mess of brown but his eyes more than make up for that. They're framed by long lashes, the irises a shade of chestnut I haven't seen before.

It's no surprise that he warrants the attention he does in the media.

Asher Foster has the number one song in the country right now. On top of that, he wrote it. I listened to it on my phone before he arrived. It's moody, soulful and surprisingly brilliant.

I look through the lens of my camera. "I need that light moved to the left."

My assistant, Remy, darts into action. She pulls it over just a touch. I'd be lost without her, especially right now, given that the small space is filled with at least ten people, all part of the entourage that arrived with the Asher.

I take another glance. It's almost perfect save for the fact that when I asked him to show me some skin, he took it to a level that's bordering on obscene.

I step around the tripod and walk back towards where he's standing in front of a pale, grey canvas hung from the ceiling.

I point towards his jeans. "You can button those back up."

He looks down. "I thought you wanted me almost naked."

He's taller than I am, but only by an inch or two. It helps that I'm wearing boots with heels today. I wouldn't have chosen this short of a skirt if I'd have known that he'd be here. I try my best to always look professional but when it's over 100 degrees outside, you have to make concessions. I'm thankful I at least took the time this morning to wash and sweep my curly brown hair up so it looks controllable.

I've already established myself as the go-to photographer for celebrities in New York City. Granted, it only constitutes part of my business, but it's the most lucrative part. I'm making enough off this shoot today to pay my rent for both the studio and my apartment for the next two months.

"It was my understanding that the photograph needed to be tasteful."

"You don't think this is tasteful." There's a low growl to his voice. "Tell me what's not tasteful about it."

The room may be milling with people, but his focus is entirely on me. I've felt that since he walked in. I imagine he's used to women taking him up on everything he offers to them. There's no denying it's tempting. I only need to look down at the top of his cock visible through the opening of his jeans to know that the man is very comfortable with his body.

"I'd prefer if you buttoned your jeans up."

"Why?" His eyes darken. "Tell me what you don't like about the way I look."

There's no way in hell this man needs his ego stroked. If that's what fuels his fire he need only turn around to where every single woman in the room, including Remy, is standing with their lips at the ready.

I've always been mildly curious about why so many women are drawn towards musicians. I don't have to wonder anymore. His confidence is undeniable but it hasn't crossed the line to cocky yet. He's just the right balance of rawness mixed with blatant aggression.

"I think I look good." He playfully nods towards his groin. "You think I look good too, don't you, Falon?"

I look around the room before I rest my hand against his shoulder and lean in just a touch. "As impressive as your dick is, I don't want it in my pictures."

Coming 2016

PREVIEW OF TENSE

A Two Part Novel Series

Featuring Nicholas Wolf

"Do you like it? Some people have said it's too long. It's actually quite thick when you're holding it in your hands, isn't it?" The tone is low and throaty, emanating somewhere from my right.

Such is the conversation on subway trains in New York City. You'd think I'd be oblivious to it all by now. Most of those who have lived here for decades have an innate ability to silence the staccato sounds of voices, traffic, and the underlying hum that is constantly hanging in the air in Manhattan.

For those of us who are considered fresh transplants, the timbres of the city are still part of its irrefutable charm. I never thought I'd get accustomed to the constant buzz of the traffic when I closed my eyes to sleep each night but now it's the lull that helps me drift off. I've only been here two years but I know that I'd long for the frenzied energy of this place if I ever decided to move back home to Florida.

"I'd like your honest opinion." I feel the slight pressure of a strong shoulder rub against mine. "Chapter seven is my personal favorite. Have you gotten that far yet?"

I glance down at the thick book resting on my lap. I know, without a doubt now, that he's talking to me. I've already had two, one-sided, conversations today about the book. One was with a woman waiting in line at the dry cleaners. The other was just fifteen minutes ago with the man who runs the bodega by my office. In both cases, I just smiled, nodded and listened to them rattle on about the awe inspiring detective novel I'm lugging around Manhattan with me.

"I haven't," I say quietly without looking at him.

No eye contact will make it easier for me to ignore him if he persists. I'm not a rude person but I do know how to protect myself with a perimeter of ignorance. Men give up easily if you pretend they don't exist. Most men do, that is. This one doesn't seem to be taking the hint.

"Have far are you?" A large hand brushes against my skirt. "You at least got past the first chapter, right?"

Physical touching is a no-no. I scoot more to my left, trying to gain even a few more inches in distance from him. This train is bursting at capacity with commuters. Part of that is the time of day and the other is the route.

It's early evening and I'm headed for Times Square, one of the few places in the city I'd be happy never seeing again. It's too much for me. There are too many people, too much noise, the smells overwhelming and the energy frenetic.

"I'm not trying to accost you." He laughs. It's a sexy growl and a few women actually turn to see the source. Judging by the way they linger when they look at him, he's not hard on the eyes.

"I'm just trying to get to a book signing," I confess, hoping he'll leave me alone if I tell him, politely, that I'm not looking to hook up. "I need to get this signed for my boss. It's a gift from his wife."

"You're hoping to meet the author? Nicholas Wolf? I heard the line for the signing was around the block already. People have been waiting all afternoon to meet him."

"Shit." I finally turn to look at his face. "You're not serious, are you?"

He's as good looking as I imagined him to be based on his voice. Seriously hot. Like seriously, I will give this man my number if he asks me for it, hot.

Black hair, blue eyes, and just the right amount of stubble on his face are the appetizer. His perfect teeth, the rugged jaw and his lips, oh those lips, are the main course. He's wearing a wool coat and jeans so who knows what dessert is, but it would be delicious. I know it would be so delicious.

"I'm serious," he says. "If you get in line now, the store is going to close before you'll get that book signed for your boss."

I roll my eyes. "I don't get the appeal. I have no idea why Gabriel likes it so much. He told me to read it so I read the first chapter and…" I point my thumb towards the floor.

"Thumbs down?" He cocks a dark winged brow. "You didn't like it?"

"It's too wordy. I was too bored to finish it."

He stares at the book before he speaks again. "I take it Gabriel is your boss? You're getting it signed for him?"

I nod sharply.

"Give it to me. I'd like to show you something."

It's not my book and since we're moving at breakneck speed inside a subway car, it's not as though he can grab it and run. I slide it from my lap to his.

"What's your name?" he asks as his hand dives into a leather bag sitting on the floor at his feet.

I watch his every movement. "Sophia. My name is Sophia. What's your name?"

He pulls a silver pen from out of the bag and before I can protest, he opens the cover of the book and starts writing.

Well, shit. I bet it's his number. I'm not going to stop him. I'll just buy another book for Mr. Foster and keep this one for me.

He closes the cover of the book, slides the pen back into his bag and turns to look at me.

"My name is Nicholas. Nicholas Wolf."

Coming Late 2016

ABOUT THE AUTHOR

Deborah Bladon has never read a romance hero she didn't like. Her love for romance novels began when she was old enough to board the bus, library card in hand to check out the newest Harlequin paperbacks. She's a Canadian by heart, and by passport, but you can often spot her in New York City sipping a latte and looking for inspiration for her next story. Manhattan is definitely her second home.

She cherishes her family and believes that each day is a gift for writing, for reading, and for loving.

16215321R00086

Printed in Great Britain
by Amazon